# Greedy Groundhogs

YEARLING BOOKS are designed especially to entertain and enlighten young people. Patricia Reilly Giff, consultant to this series, received her bachelor's degree from Marymount College and a master's degree in history from St. John's University. She holds a Professional Diploma in Reading and a Doctorate of Humane Letters from Hofstra University. She was a teacher and reading consultant for many years, and is the author of numerous books for young readers.

# Greedy Groundhogs

## JUDY DELTON

*Illustrated by Alan Tiegreen*

A YEARLING BOOK

Published by
Bantam Doubleday Dell Books for Young Readers
a division of
Bantam Doubleday Dell Publishing Group, Inc.
1540 Broadway
New York, New York 10036

ISBN: 0-440-40931-4

Printed in the United States of America

February 1994

10 9 8 7 6 5

CWO

For Karen Carlson, in Hastings, Minnesota,
who keeps children reading and authors writing

# Contents

1 A Furry Badge     1

2 The Badgeless Badge     15

3 Soap Talk     25

4 No Groundhog Yet     40

5 Bigger than a Basement     56

6 Close Enough     65

7 Seven Letters Meaning Fun     75

# CHAPTER 1

# A Furry Badge

"What keeps a house warm?" asked Tracy Barnes.

"The sun," said Tim Noon.

"Fire," said Sonny Stone.

"Dummy," said Roger White. "Fire would warm your house all right. It would burn it down to the ground!"

"Would not," said Sonny.

"Would too," said Roger.

"How many letters does it have?" asked Rachel Meyers.

Tracy counted the little boxes in her crossword puzzle. "Seven," she said.

"What letters do you have?" asked Kevin Moe.

"Just the first one," said Tracy. "It's an *F*."

"Fireplace!" shouted Sonny. "I told you so!"

"Fireplace has nine letters, not seven," said Kenny Baker.

"It's simple," said Tim Noon. "Furnace."

"Rat's knees!" said Molly Duff. "Why didn't I think of that?"

Molly was seven years old. She was in second grade. And she was a Pee Wee Scout. Troop 23 met in their leader's basement on Tuesday afternoons. Their leader's name was Mrs. Peters.

Molly was glad it was Tim who had known the answer. He was quiet and usually didn't say much. Kevin was the one who knew the most answers. Molly liked Kevin. She wanted to marry him when she grew up. Kevin had lots of ambition. He wanted to be mayor of their town someday.

Tracy wrote *E R N A S E* in the blank spaces following the *F*.

"That's wrong," said Kevin, looking over her shoulder.

He erased the first *E* and put in a *U*.

Then he erased the *S* and put in a *C*.

On the cover of Tracy's book it said *101 Easy Crossword Puzzles.*

"I don't think these are easy," said Tracy. "My aunt gave me this book. She said if I did all these puzzles it would help me with my spelling."

"Spelling," said baby Nick. He repeated things the Pee Wees said. He was Mrs. Peters's baby.

Mrs. Peters passed out big pieces of paper. She passed out some crayons.

"Today," she said, "we are going to talk about the new badges we are going to earn this month. It is only late January but spring is coming."

"Spring!" shouted Nick. "Spring, spring, spring!"

"In February the groundhog, who has

been hibernating all winter, comes out of his hole."

"What's 'hibernating'?" asked Tim.

"Who can answer Tim's question?" asked Mrs. Peters.

"Why doesn't *she* answer it?" whispered Mary Beth Kelly to Molly. Mary Beth was Molly's best friend.

Molly often thought it would save a lot of time if teachers and scout leaders would answer those hard questions themselves instead of asking children who did not know.

"I think they learn that in scout leaders' school," Molly whispered back. "They must tell them not to answer questions. They must say 'Ask the Pee Wees first.' "

Hands were waving.

"It means cooking," shouted Patty Baker. She was Kenny's twin sister. "It's like barbecuing. Groundhogs cook in the winter. And the stove keeps them warm too," she added.

5

Roger burst into laughter. "Ho, ho, ho," he said. "That's a good one. 'Hibernating' doesn't mean cooking. It means digging. Groundhogs dig deeper holes in winter."

Mrs. Peters frowned. "Not exactly," she said politely. "They may do that, but it is not what 'hibernating' means."

More hands waved.

"It means thinking," said Kenny Baker. "Groundhogs think in winter because there's nothing else for them to do."

Tracy looked disgusted. " 'Hibernating' means they have babies," she said. "I should know, my aunt is hibernating all the time and she had four babies."

Tracy and Kenny began to argue over who was right. Lisa Ronning said, " 'Hibernating' means eating too much. Groundhogs eat all the nuts they collect in fall."

"It's squirrels that gather nuts in fall," said Mary Beth. "Not groundhogs!"

Finally Mrs. Peters raised her hands in the air and said, "Quiet, please! 'Hibernate' means to spend the winter in a sleeplike state. Groundhogs sleep all winter long."

"I knew that," said Rachel.

"So did I," said Kevin.

"Mrs. Peters sounds mad," said Mary Beth.

"She should answer her questions herself," said Molly.

Mrs. Peters drew a picture of a groundhog on the blackboard. She drew his hole beside him. Then, underneath the picture, below the earth, she drew many tunnels.

"The groundhog digs lots and lots of tunnels. At the end of one of them he or she builds a nest of grass. When winter comes, the groundhog crawls into the nest and stays there until spring."

"What's this got to do with our badge?" shouted Sonny.

"Just wait," said Mrs. Peters, "and I'll tell you.

"As I said, when winter is almost over the groundhog comes out of his hole and looks around. Legend has it that if it is sunny when he comes out in February and he sees his shadow, he's frightened and crawls back into his nest to sleep some more and we have six more weeks of winter. If it is a cloudy day and he can't see his shadow, the groundhog comes out of his hole, signaling that spring is on the way."

Mrs. Peters erased the tunnels on the blackboard and wrote down some things that groundhogs like to eat.

"Groundhogs are members of the marmot family. They love to eat grass and clover and corn from farmers' fields," she said. "And they eat nuts and other growing things, but they do not eat other animals. They are vegetarians."

"So is my uncle!" shouted Lisa.

But Mrs. Peters was not finished talking about groundhogs.

"Their tunnels can be as long as this room," she said. "And they can be as deep in the ground as the height of a person."

The Pee Wees looked around the room.

Roger whistled a long, low whistle. "That's a lot for one fuzzball to dig," he said.

Mrs. Peters nodded. "Just one groundhog can move a million tons of dirt in his lifetime."

The Pee Wees stopped to think about that.

"No way," said Roger.

No one else doubted their leader's words. "How does he know?" whispered Molly to Mary Beth. "He thinks he's so smart."

"In May the groundhog has babies, but they are very often killed by cars or hunters or the red fox," said Mrs. Peters. "Groundhog meat is supposed to taste good, although few people know that."

"Yuck!" said Rachel, holding on to her throat. "Who could eat such a cute little furry thing?"

Now all the Pee Wees were making choking noises, and pretending to be sick.

Mrs. Peters had to hold up her hand again.

"Another name for the groundhog is 'woodchuck.' The word 'woodchuck' comes from the Cree Indian word 'wuchak,' " she said.

Kevin asked some questions about woodchucks. So did Rachel.

"I know more than I want to know about groundhogs now," said Sonny. "Who cares?"

"I think nature is very interesting," said Rachel. "I may be a scientist and study marmots. Or at least I'll be a veterinarian."

"Now, on your papers," said Mrs. Peters, "I want you to draw a picture of a groundhog."

The Pee Wees all picked up their crayons.

"They are fairly small animals," said their leader, "with a bushy tail and short legs. They are usually a brown color."

Molly got out her brown crayon.

"I'm going to put mine up in a tree," said Tim.

"They can't climb trees, dummy," said Roger. "Can they, Mrs. Peters?"

"Yes, they can climb," said their leader. "And they can also swim. They keep busy playing in rocks and fields all day and sleeping at night, just like you do."

The Pee Wees laughed. Tim held up his picture. "Here's mine in a tree," he said. Rachel drew her groundhog in a real bed instead of a nest of grass. Sonny drew his groundhog with a red swimsuit on.

"So what do we have to do for this badge?" demanded Roger. "Do we have to go hunting for a groundhog and make soup out of him?"

"Do we have to trap one?" asked Kenny.

"Do we have to dig one up?" asked Sonny.

"I'm not going to touch one," said Rachel. "They must be full of dirt after digging a tunnel as long as this room."

"And fleas," added Patty.

"You don't have to do any of those things," said Mrs. Peters, laughing. "I'll tell you what to do as soon as all of you finish your pictures."

# CHAPTER 2

# The Badgeless Badge

After all the pictures were finished, Mrs. Peters held up a badge. It had a furry brown animal on it, made of fuzzy fabric. He had tiny ears and whiskers. He looked soft to pet. Molly wanted that badge. She didn't care what she had to do to earn it! (Except, of course, if she had to eat fried groundhog. But Mrs. Peters would never ask the Pee Wees to do that!)

"What I want you to do for this badge is go to the library and find out as much as you can about groundhogs. Keep a little notebook and write down their food, their habits, and other things that are interesting."

15

"That's easy," said Mary Beth.

"It's a snap," said Molly. "This will be the easiest badge we ever got!" Molly could picture it on her blouse already!

"I'm not finished," said their leader. "The other thing I want you to do is watch for the groundhog to come out of his hole and look for his shadow. See if you can spot a groundhog, and follow it and see if he casts a shadow or not. If he does not cast a shadow we will know that spring is on the way."

"I think it would be a lot easier just to wait till the tulips and crocuses come up to know it is spring," said Rachel. "Or just look at the calendar. It won't be easy to find a groundhog hole if it snows."

"Their holes are about one foot across the top," said Mrs. Peters. "So they will be easy to see."

Rachel was right, thought Molly. How could all the Pee Wees be in the right place when the groundhog decided to stick his head out of his tunnel?

What if it was early in the morning on a Saturday or Sunday, before they were out of bed?

What if it was late at night when it was dark, or when they were in school or eating dinner or at the dentist's?

Tulips seemed a much better sign of spring. They stayed around longer and didn't pop back into the ground if they saw their shadows.

"February second is Groundhog Day," said Mrs. Peters. "But you can start watching for him anytime."

"Do we have to actually see a groundhog in order to get the badge?" asked Rachel.

"That would be the best way to get the badge," said their leader.

She didn't say what the worst way was, thought Molly. In fact she didn't say any other way except the library books.

While the Pee Wees were thinking about this, Sonny's mother, Mrs. Stone, brought down hot chocolate with marshmallows in it. She was the assistant scout leader.

Sonny was still drawing. He was putting a red beach jacket on his groundhog to match its swimsuit. Lisa was putting nail polish on her groundhog's tiny toenails.

After the cocoa and some homemade cookies the scouts sang their Pee Wee Scout song and said their Pee Wee pledge. Then they did some indoor exercises and told about some good deeds.

"Now," said Mrs. Peters, "I want to tell you what else we are going to do this month. It isn't something we'll get a badge for, but it's something to keep us busy during long winter days."

The Pee Wees groaned. Activities with no badge were no fun.

"We don't do things just for badges," said Mrs. Peters, reading their minds. "We do

things because they make us better people and better citizens and because they help others."

The Pee Wees groaned again. Being better people did not sound like fun.

"These long winter days give us lots of time to do things. And one of the things it would be fun to do is something to improve our homes."

"My home doesn't need improvement, Mrs. Peters," said Tracy. "It's brand new."

"Every home can use something to make it more comfortable," said their leader. "Maybe you could make a book rack for your room with a few milk cartons. Or you could help your dad paint the walls in your room."

"I don't have any dad, Mrs. Peters," shouted Tim.

"I don't either," called out Lisa. "My dad left us last year."

"I don't have my own room," said Mary

Beth. "My sister wouldn't let me paint my half of the room."

"You can help your mom paint too," said Mrs. Peters.

More hands waved.

"Or your sister, or your aunt or uncle."

The hands went down.

"Tonight you can think about something simple you can do that will be a nice winter project."

"Can't we get a groundhog badge *and* a winter project badge?" asked Kevin. Two badges! Molly liked that idea. "Now, let's not be greedy," said Mrs. Peters, smiling.

"We need another bedroom in our house," said Lisa. "Maybe I can put one on."

All the scouts laughed.

They all pretended to hammer and saw and put up a new wall in Mrs. Peters's basement.

"You need blueprints and levels and shingles and all that stuff," said Kevin. "You can't put a room on your house alone."

"That is very thoughtful," said Mrs. Peters, "but you will have to try something a little easier. Earning the groundhog badge and improving your home will be a good thing to think about while we wait for spring."

After the meeting there was lots of talk about the projects. Molly did not know where to find a groundhog or what she could do for her house.

"I'm going to plant seeds in milk cartons and when they grow it will be spring and I can put the plants in our garden," said Rachel. "I'm going to plant tomatoes, and my mom can make salads and she can preserve some that are left over."

Molly looked at Rachel. How could she have everything planned already? Right down to the tomato salads. Molly wished she could plan that fast. And think of something that good to do. There was no room in her yard for tomatoes.

"I'm going to think of something better than any of you guys," said Tim.

Molly felt sorry for Tim. His family was poor and sometimes they didn't have enough food. Molly hoped he would make something they needed. Both Tim and Sonny often had big ideas that did not work out. Sonny was a baby and the others laughed at him. Molly felt as if she had to protect Sonny and Tim and help them with projects that failed.

"I think looking for groundhogs is more important than doing that unbadge thing," said Tracy. "We get a badge for groundhogs. I don't want to work hard for nothing."

Molly hated to admit she felt the same way. If she was going to work hard she wanted a badge for it. But Mrs. Peters had warned them about doing things for badges instead of for people.

"Maybe this is a test," said Mary Beth. "To see if we can do something for nothing!"

"I'm going to spend more time on the

home thing than on the groundhogs," said Lisa. "Groundhogs aren't that important."

"Well, I want that badge," said Molly.

"I do too," said Mary Beth.

One thing was for certain. No one wanted to be the only Pee Wee without that furry animal badge. Not even Lisa.

# CHAPTER 3

# Soap Talk

On the way home Molly and Mary Beth stopped at the library for some books about groundhogs. Molly wanted to read all about them. Especially where you had to go to see one come out of its hole.

But when they got to the library all the Pee Wees were there. And all the groundhog books were gone.

Sonny and Roger were fighting over a big book with a groundhog on the cover.

"I saw it first!" shouted Sonny.

"Did not!" said Roger, pulling harder.

"Give me that book!" said Sonny, giving

25

Roger a big shove. Roger got angry and gave the book a big pull and Sonny a harder shove. Sonny let go and went toppling over. He fell into a tall wooden stand that had a fern on top of it.

Molly ran to try to catch the fern, but it was too late. It sailed off the stand and came down right on Sonny's head, spilling dirt in all directions.

The crash of Sonny, the pot, and the stand falling made such a racket that everyone in the library stared.

The librarian, whose name was Mrs. Winkle, did more than stare. She came marching over to Sonny, and her face did not look as friendly as a librarian's face should look.

She helped Sonny up and brushed him off. Then she took Sonny and Roger into her little office. As Molly and Mary Beth listened they could hear a few words like "A library is no place to wrestle," and

". . . come here to read quietly," and ". . . notify your teacher and parents if this happens again."

"Pee Wees aren't supposed to get into trouble," said Mary Beth in disgust. "Roger and Sonny could give us all a bad name."

Mrs. Winkle came out of her office. Her face was red and she announced to the Pee Wees that there were not very many books about groundhogs.

"You will just have to share them," she said. "Some of you can read them here, and the others can take them home."

The Pee Wees sat down at a big table and read. Molly shared a book with Mary Beth.

Rachel announced that she was going to the adult section to get a nature book.

The girls read their book, but did not learn much more than Mrs. Peters had told them.

"Let's go," said Mary Beth. "It doesn't tell where to watch for them. It's up to us to find out for ourselves."

The girls said good-bye at the corner, and Molly went home to her room and hung up her picture of the groundhog. Then she sat down at the little desk her father had built, to make a list of things she could do for her un-badge. For the house. It made Molly feel good to make lists.

But this time she couldn't think of a thing to write. She ate dinner and got ready for bed and still she had nothing on her list.

The next afternoon after school Molly and Mary Beth walked up one street and down another, looking for the groundhog.

"We have no idea where he lives," groaned Mary Beth. "And if we did, we still wouldn't know when he's coming out."

"We just have to keep looking," said Molly.

Up and down. Up and down.

Up one alley. Down two streets.

Behind the school. In the front yard of the courthouse.

"I don't think groundhogs live downtown," said Molly. "There are too many stores and not enough ground like lawns and gardens."

"They probably live in the country," said Molly. "Mrs. Peters said they like cornfields, and there are no cornfields in town."

The girls walked to the edge of town. The houses grew farther and farther apart. There was more grass. There were more trees. But there were no cornfields.

"Let's look for holes," said Mary Beth. "Mrs. Peters says his hole is a foot across."

"Whose foot?" said Molly. "Ours, or Roger's?"

"Or our dads'," said Mary Beth. "My dad wears size fourteen shoes. That's huge!" She showed Molly with her hands.

The girls walked up and down, up and down, looking for big holes. Up one hill. Down the other side.

Across one field. Back across another.

Eyes to the ground.

"Here is a hole!" called Molly, pointing.

Mary Beth scrambled over.

"That's a hole some machine made," she said. "Or the wheel of a car where it got stuck. It's not a groundhog hole."

Farther on was another hole.

"That's where someone was walking," said Molly. "It's the shape of a boot. Groundhogs don't wear boots!"

Sure enough, nearby the girls found the old boot that someone had lost when it got stuck in the mud.

Soon the sky got dark and the girls started for home.

"What a wasted afternoon," grumbled Mary Beth. "We could have been working on our unbadge thing."

Molly felt like crying. She couldn't find a groundhog. And she couldn't think of anything to make for her house.

"I'm going to make a soap dish for our bathroom," said Mary Beth. "Out of clay. I have to make it and bake it and glaze it. It takes a lot of time."

"Rat's knees!" said Molly. "I wish I could think of something."

"Make a soap dish like mine," said Mary Beth.

It was tempting to work with her best friend. But Molly wanted something different. Something of her own that no one else was making. She didn't like to be a copycat.

"Maybe I could make soap to put in it," said Molly. "My grandma used to make soap."

Molly's mother liked to put fancy little bars of soap in the guest bathroom. Soap in the shape of little shells. Maybe Molly could make those little shells and her mother wouldn't have to buy them!

"What goes in soap?" she asked Mary Beth.

"I don't know," said her friend. "But you could collect all those old little pieces of soap that are left in the dish, that your mom throws out. We could melt them down."

Molly liked the sound of the word "we."

"Would it be cheating to use old soap to make new?" she asked.

"I don't think so," said Mary Beth. "Everything starts with something. You can't make soap out of air."

That made sense. Mary Beth was always sensible.

Molly began to get excited about this project. Once she had some little soaps to show Mrs. Peters, she'd have her unbadge behind her. Then she could spend all the time on groundhogs!

"When can we start?" she asked her friend.

"How about Saturday morning?" said Mary Beth.

"Fine," said Molly. "I'll get the soap by then."

After Molly's bath that evening, her mother put a new bar of soap in the soap dish and

Molly took the little used one and popped it into a bag in her closet.

The next day at school Mary Beth handed her three more.

"I got them from the girls' lavatory," she said.

By Saturday Molly had plenty. She went to Mary Beth's garage, where she found her friend painting her soap dish.

Mary Beth looked into the bag. "You can't carve it into shells like it is," she said. "We'll have to melt it down with some hot water."

What a smart friend! And what a big help! The girls ran in and got a pot of hot water. They dumped the old soap in and stirred it.

"It's still there," said Molly, looking in.

"We have to stir it harder," said Mary Beth.

The girls got sticks from a shelf in the garage and stirred and stirred. Faster and faster and faster. As they stirred, bubbles began to form. The faster they stirred, the faster the bubbles rose in the pot! Pretty soon the

bubbles ran over the top and out onto the floor!

Underneath the bubbles was soapy water.

"This doesn't look like something we can carve into shells," said Molly, looking deep into the pot.

"We have to leave it to get hard," said Mary Beth. "It has to set like jelly."

The girls went for a walk. They stopped to visit Sonny, who was giving one of the young twins a bottle of juice.

And they stopped at Lisa's, where she was trying to decide on an unbadge project.

At Rachel's they looked at her little rows of seeds planted in milk cartons filled with soil.

"Now the soap will be hard," said Molly as they ran back to the garage.

But it wasn't. "What makes stuff hard?" asked Molly.

"My mom makes salads hard with Jell-O," Mary Beth said.

"And it will make it a better color too!" said Molly. "Jell-O will do both things!"

Molly ran home and took a package of cherry Jell-O from the pantry shelf. She would tell her mom later, after she saw the soap.

The girls poured the Jell-O into the pot and stirred it. "It says it takes an hour to set," said Molly.

Molly helped Mary Beth paint her soap dish. Then they went into the house and watched cartoons on TV. After that they played Monopoly in Mary Beth's room. By the time they finished, two hours had gone by.

"Now!" said Molly. "I hope the soap isn't *too* hard!"

It wasn't. It was the same as before, only bright pink.

"Rat's knees," said Molly sadly. "We can't carve this."

The girls stared into the pink soup with bubbles.

"We can't waste it," said Mary Beth. "Maybe you can give it to your mom to wash clothes in instead. Like liquid detergent."

"Not with Jell-O in it," said Molly. "It would make the clothes pink."

Mary Beth poured the pink soup into the garden in the backyard. Molly's project was gone.

# CHAPTER 4

# No Groundhog Yet

"There are better things than making soap," said Mary Beth sensibly.

"Like what?" asked Molly.

Mary Beth thought. "Well, just about anything," she said. "You'll think of something good. You're creative."

It was true. Molly's parents often told her she had a wild imagination. But a wild imagination was a lot of work.

Tuesday was coming again, and it would be time for the next Pee Wee Scout meeting. Molly hated to go. She had no groundhog and no home project.

On Tuesday when Molly got to Mrs. Peters's house, she saw Sonny dragging a long pole down the sidewalk. Well, at least Sonny had a project. She would not have to worry about helping him. She had to help herself instead.

Inside, Rachel was setting her tiny plants on the table. Kenny Baker had carved his family name into a piece of wood to hang over the mailbox.

Mary Beth had her soap dish and Roger had a knife holder. Mrs. Peters was admiring the unbadge things.

Sonny picked up his long pole to tell about it. It was so long that it hit the ceiling light in their leader's basement.

*Crash!* went the pole.

"You broke the light!" yelled Roger.

The Pee Wees all looked at Mrs. Peters. She looked upset but not angry. Their leader did not get angry with her scouts. Not very often.

"It was an accident," she said, getting a

broom and dustpan to sweep up the glass. "All of you stay seated so you don't get cut."

"Sonny made a light breaker," said Roger. "Ho, ho, ho, that's a good thing to have around the house, Stone!"

"It's not a light breaker," said Sonny. "You put a rag on the end of this pole and you can wash high-up windows. Or roofs."

"Or light bulbs!" said Rachel, smiling.

Soon everything was in order again, and Mrs. Peters took Sonny's pole outside.

"Just in case," she said.

Kevin came in later with the best unbadge thing so far. It was a sewing box for his mother. It had a little door that opened and shut with a *click*.

"Now, how many of you have seen a groundhog?" asked Mrs. Peters.

Several hands waved.

"They're lying," said Mary Beth. "Molly and I looked and looked and didn't see one."

"Well, it could have been a beaver," admitted Roger. "It was building a dam in the creek by my house."

"Groundhogs don't build dams," said Rachel.

"Well, keep an eye out," said Mrs. Peters, laughing. "Remember, the groundhog likes sun. He will come out during the day, when his nest feels too warm. You should be ready to watch him.

"Maybe you can put some food out in the yard to attract him. He would like to have a fine ear of corn."

After the meeting, when the scouts got outside, Sonny said, "I saw my groundhog. I'll get my badge right off."

"Why didn't you tell Mrs. Peters? And where did you see a groundhog?" asked Tracy.

"I'm not telling," said Sonny. "He's mine. You find your own."

"You can't own a groundhog, dummy,"

said Tracy. "He belongs to all of us. Where is he?"

"He lives in my yard, so he's my groundhog," said Sonny.

The Pee Wees raced over to Sonny's house. They looked all over the yard.

"There he is, eating that old acorn," said Sonny.

The Pee Wees looked. Sure enough, there on the branch of an oak tree was something eating an acorn. But it was no groundhog.

"That's a squirrel!" cried Molly. "Don't you know a squirrel from a groundhog?"

"What a baby," said Mary Beth.

"Maybe Sonny needs glasses," said Molly. She wondered if she should mention this to his mother. She hated to see everyone make fun of Sonny.

"We'll find our own groundhog," said Tracy. "And he won't be a squirrel."

Pretty soon all the Pee Wees had left Sonny's except Molly, Rachel, and Tim.

"Can you come and look for a groundhog with me?" Molly asked Rachel. Lately she did everything with Mary Beth. Maybe it was time to change her habits.

"I saw my groundhog," said Rachel. "At least I think it was a groundhog. It was in my aunt's backyard. It was gray and it came out of a hole. My aunt said it was close enough."

"You mean you aren't sure either?" said Molly. "Maybe you saw a squirrel, like Sonny."

"Well, it could have been a mouse, I guess, but it was pretty big for a mouse."

Rat's knees. Molly didn't want a mouse that looked like a groundhog. She didn't want a squirrel that looked like a groundhog. She wanted a real groundhog! If she got a badge she wanted to get it fair and square.

Rachel said good-bye and started home. Sonny was in the house watching TV.

"I know where groundhogs live," said Tim to Molly. "There are woods in my backyard, and I'm going to dig a great big hole way down to the tunnels."

"I don't think that's very nice," said Molly, "to dig his house up."

"It's the only way to find the thing," said Tim.

Maybe Tim was right.

"You can help me if you want," he said. "It's a lot of digging for one person. Then we can both get our badges when we find him."

Molly thought about it. She didn't have any better ideas.

"Okay," she said. "I'll come over after school tomorrow."

"Come alone," warned Tim. "This is our groundhog."

On the way home Molly remembered that Mrs. Peters had not asked her about her un-badge project. She was safe until the next meeting. By that time she'd think of something. Meanwhile, she and Tim would dig.

The next afternoon when school was out,

Tim whispered, "Don't walk with me! I don't want anyone to know we are working together."

Molly sighed. Here she was helping Tim out and he didn't even appreciate it. She took a shortcut to Tim's and was there before he was.

They went through the yard and behind an old garage and past some tall trees.

Tim pointed. "He's under there," he said. He handed Molly a shovel from the garage and took one himself. "Let's get going," he said. "We have a lot to do."

"Does your mother know what you're doing?" asked Molly.

"Not if you don't tell her," he replied. "No one comes back here behind these trees."

The dirt was hard. The shovel was crooked. It took ages to dig even a little hole. After they had been digging for a half hour Molly said, "We need more help."

"No way," said Tim.

"Then I'm going home," said Molly.

Tim must have realized he could not dig a deep hole alone, so he said, "Okay. Who should we ask?"

"The more people the better," said Molly.

She went home and called the other Pee Wees. Tracy had an allergist's appointment. Lisa had a piano lesson. Sonny said no.

But some of the others came over right away. They all were anxious to dig for groundhogs. Each brought a shovel, and before long there was a bigger hole in Tim's backyard.

"Be careful you don't hit my groundhog on the head," yelled Tim.

"Mrs. Peters said their tunnels are as long as her basement," sighed Rachel. "This could take forever."

The Pee Wees dug and dug. And then they dug some more.

They did not see a tunnel. They did not see a nest. They did not see a groundhog.

"This is the hardest badge we've ever earned," said Mary Beth, collapsing on the brown grass to rest.

"This is a big hole, and I don't see a groundhog yet," said Kenny.

"Maybe he won't come out because he sees us," said Rachel. "He is probably just going deeper and deeper to get away from us."

If Rachel was right (and she usually was) it was silly to keep digging.

"Maybe we should leave some food out to try to tempt him," said Kevin. "That's what Mrs. Peters told us to do."

That did make more sense than digging, thought Molly.

"Have you got any groundhog food?" Kevin asked Tim.

Tim ran into the house and came out with a banana, a Twinkie, and part of a dough-nut.

The others rushed home and found some

cereal and pizza and one piece of fudge. Patty came back with some ginger ale in a paper cup.

"In case he's thirsty," she said.

"This isn't exactly groundhog food," said Kevin.

"It's better than groundhog food," said Tim. "It's people food. Any animal likes people food."

Tim was right, thought Molly. Lucky, Mrs. Peters's mascot dog, loved it when he could share a Pee Wee cupcake. What groundhog could turn down pepperoni pizza?

The Pee Wees put the food out on paper plates that Patty had brought. Then they hid in the garage for ten minutes. When they came out, the food was still there.

"Rat's knees!" said Molly. "We will have to leave it overnight. We can look tomorrow and I'll bet we'll see him eating breakfast."

The Pee Wees sighed and started home. They were all bone tired. This badge was

definitely not easy. And it was definitely not fast.

But nothing hard had ever stopped the Pee Wee Scouts.

# CHAPTER 5

# Bigger than a Basement

"**Y**ou look all tuckered out!" said Molly's mother when Molly got home.

"And you look like you have been digging to China!" said her dad.

Molly wondered if her dad knew how close to the truth he came.

Molly took her bath before dinner. After dinner she was going to think about ground-hogs. And the unbadge. And what to do about both of them. Instead, she fell asleep.

No one was up in time to check Tim's back-yard before school. But after school all the Pee Wees were there.

"Some of the food is gone!" said Tim.

"But we didn't see who ate it," said Rachel. "It could have been a squirrel or a rabbit."

"All our digging was wasted," sighed Mary Beth.

"All that work for nothing," agreed Molly.

"Tim could plant a garden," said Rachel.

"That won't get me the dumb groundhog badge," Tim said.

That night it rained hard.

Molly could hear the drops beat against her windows.

In the morning Molly wore her raincoat over a sweater to school. Tim was on the playground waiting for her. He was smiling.

"I've got the best unbadge house thing of all," he told her. "Better than Sonny's dumb pole and better than Rachel's garden or Kevin's sewing box."

"What is it?" asked Molly.

"I'm not telling. It's a surprise."

"Are you bringing it to our scout meeting on Tuesday?" asked Molly.

"I can't. It's too big. It's bigger than any-one's. It's bigger than my basement!"

"Rat's knees, tell me!" demanded Molly.

"Come over after school and bring all the Pee Wees," he said.

After school the Pee Wees scrambled to get to the Noons' house first.

"What do you think it is?" asked Mary Beth.

"I don't know, but I hope it's something his family can use," said Molly.

When they got there Tim was waiting. He led them back to the place where they had dug for groundhogs.

"Look!" he said, pointing.

The Pee Wees looked.

"There's water in the hole we dug," said Roger. "So what?"

Tim stamped his foot. "That's not just wa-ter," he said. "That's my swimming pool! I'll bet no one else made a swimming pool for their house!"

58

The Pee Wees had to admit, no one had.

After a little while Rachel said, "I think swimming pools have cement in the bottom."

"Don't need it," said Tim.

"My uncle's pool has a deck around it, with lawn chairs and umbrellas," said Mary Beth.

"I've got umbrellas," said Tim. "I'll put chairs and umbrellas next to it when I'm ready. I told you mine was bigger than a basement!"

Molly felt like laughing, but at least Tim had something for his house, she thought. She had nothing!

"Come over tomorrow and bring your swimsuits," said Tim.

"Ha, Noon, I'm not diving in that mud," said Roger. "Besides, it's too cold. We'll get pneumonia!"

Tim looked like he would cry.

"I'll come!" said Molly. She hated to hurt Tim's feelings. She didn't think her mother would approve, but she could put her swimsuit on under her clothes. If it was too cold she could swim with her jacket on!

"So will I," said Mary Beth, feeling sorry for Tim.

The rest of the Pee Wees finally agreed that they would come.

The next day the sun was out and it was warmer. But not warm enough to swim, Roger said.

"This is really dumb," said Rachel on the way to Tim's.

"It's not dumb if it makes Tim feel good," said Molly.

The Pee Wees ran to Tim's backyard and took off their jackets and clothes. They were shivering in their swimsuits as they lined up along the edge of his pool. But when they were ready to jump in and swim, they noticed something. The water was gone! There was no pool. There was just a hole in the ground.

Tim was sitting in an old lawn chair under

an umbrella that had blown inside out. He was crying.

"It's gone," he cried. "My pool is gone."

"Water soaks into the ground," said Rachel. "You need concrete."

"The sun came out and dried it up," said Kevin.

Tim threw himself on the ground and moaned. The Pee Wees tried to cheer him up, but he got up and ran inside his house and slammed the door. The Pee Wees took their beach towels and started for home.

Molly felt terrible. Tim had no project, and neither did she.

"What's a three-letter word that means Santa's helper?" asked Tracy on the way home.

Molly was in no mood to think of crosswords for Tracy. She had other things on her mind. Important things.

"I wish she'd finish that book her aunt gave her," grumbled Mary Beth.

"It will take years," said Molly. "It's really thick and she hasn't done very many."

"What's a Santa's helper?" Tracy repeated.

"Elf," said Molly. "That's simple."

Tracy wrote it in.

All of a sudden Molly stopped and stood as still as a statue.

"Look!" she whispered, pointing. "Look what is under that tree in the park!"

# CHAPTER 6
## Close Enough

The Pee Wees did not move. They saw an animal standing next to a tree.

He was a brownish color.

He had a bushy tail.

He had small ears and whiskers.

"It's him!" shouted Sonny. "It's my groundhog!"

"Shh," whispered Molly. "You'll scare him away."

"There's no shadow!" whispered Mary Beth.

There was no spot on the ground beside the groundhog. "He is standing there! It must be spring!" Lisa said excitedly.

"It might not be a groundhog," said Kevin reasonably.

"It might be a squirrel," said Roger. "I've seen a brown squirrel before."

"It's a groundhog," said Mary Beth firmly. "It's the same shape as in the picture in the encyclopedia."

Some of the Pee Wees wrote in their notebooks. Molly wrote down the day and the time and the place and what he looked like. Then she drew a little picture.

She finished her notes just in time. Kenny stepped on a twig and it made a snapping noise. The groundhog ran down into his hole.

"Rat's knees!" shouted Molly. "We did it! We saw the groundhog. Everyone but Tim saw it."

"It may not have been a groundhog," said Roger. "We didn't get close enough to tell."

The other Pee Wees all sprang on him.

"Of course it was!" said Tracy.

"It was brown and had a bushy tail," said Rachel.

"It was eating corn," said Molly.

Roger walked over to the tree. He picked something up.

"This is an old cookie," he said. "It doesn't say in the book that groundhogs eat cookies."

Molly stamped her foot. "No book lists every kind of food that a groundhog will eat," she said. "If you show a groundhog a cookie he'll eat it."

But some of the Pee Wees were doubtful.

"We can never be positively sure," said Molly, frowning at Roger.

"No groundhog is going to wear a little sign around his neck, saying I AM A GROUNDHOG," said Rachel.

"You can't prove it's a real one," said Roger.

"You can't prove it isn't!" said Lisa back.

"I say it's a groundhog," said Mary Beth.

"And I say if it isn't, it's close enough," said Molly.

Right now Molly was tired of looking and a "make do" groundhog was all right with her. But she knew this one was real. And if it wasn't, it was close enough.

The Pee Wees all started for home. Molly and Mary Beth walked together.

"Too bad Tim didn't see it," said Molly.

"You know, it could have been a squirrel," said Mary Beth.

"It was a groundhog," said Molly loudly. "And that's that."

Molly ran to her house. She was glad to have the groundhog behind her. She could get the badge with the others. Now if only she had her unbadge!

As she ran up her front steps her mother was coming out to shake the rugs.

"It's spring!" said Molly to her mother. "We saw a groundhog outside!"

Her mother smiled. "Good," she said. "It

feels like spring. If we had a barbecue grill I'd make our supper on it tonight!"

Her mother's words gave Molly an idea. A grill was something for the house. It was something her family could use. Where could she get one?

Molly ran into the house and called Rachel. Rachel knew about a lot of things. She told Rachel her problem.

"I have an idea," Rachel said. "I'll be right over."

When she got there she said, "You know, a barbecue grill is just a big pan with something on top to put the hot dogs on."

The girls ran to the garage. There were loose boards and rakes and scraps of metal.

"What's this?" demanded Rachel. She picked up an old trash-can cover. "It would be a good barbecue! And I know what to put on top. Follow me."

The girls went over to Rachel's house. They ran down into her basement.

"Here!" she said. Rachel held up an old oven rack. "It's from our old stove," she said. "I'll ask my mom if we can take it."

"Yes," said Mrs. Meyers. "We don't have that stove anymore."

The girls dashed back to Molly's, and Rachel set the rack on top of the trash-can cover. "You put the charcoal right under here," said Rachel.

"It's perfect," said Molly. She threw her arms around her friend and thanked her.

"I wish I had thought of that," said Rachel. "But we have a gas barbecue in the backyard. I guess we don't need a charcoal one too."

After Rachel left, Molly took the rack and cover down to the basement and washed them. When her dad came home from work she ran and showed her parents.

"Do you need this cover for anything?" asked Molly.

"I think we need it for our supper!" said her dad, smiling. "I'll get some charcoal and try it out!"

"What an imagination you have," said her mother. "We just talked about the grill and here it is ready to use tonight!"

Mr. Duff came home from the store with charcoal and hot dogs. He set the grill on some piled-up rocks in the backyard. He made a fire and the family roasted their hot dogs on Molly's grill. Molly roasted her hot dog on a long stick over the grill so she could pretend she was at a campfire.

"Yum," said Molly. "These taste like a picnic."

"The first one of the year, thanks to Molly!" said her dad.

Molly was tired out from the long day's work. She fell asleep as soon as she got into bed. She had no more badges or unbadges to worry about for now. She only wished that

Tim had been with them when they had seen the groundhog. And that he had something for his house instead of the pool without water.

# CHAPTER 7

# Seven Letters
# Meaning Fun

At the meeting on Tuesday there was a lot of bumping and banging. And clinging and clanging. Some of the noise was Molly's grill bumping around in a big plastic bag.

But first of all Mrs. Peters wanted to hear groundhog news. And everyone could give it.

"It was brown and had a bushy tail," shouted Lisa.

"It had small ears and whiskers and it didn't see its own shadow," said Patty.

"It could have been a squirrel," said Roger.

The Pee Wees all made a dive for Roger. Arms and legs flew. There was some scrambling on the floor.

Mrs. Peters held her hand up.

She waited until they all sat down again.

"I'm sure it was a groundhog," she said. "It sounds just like one."

"And if it wasn't, it was close enough," said Rachel.

"Too bad Tim didn't see him," whispered Mary Beth.

But Tim was waving something in the air.

"Mrs. Peters!" he shouted. "I took a picture of my groundhog. He was in my swimming pool."

So Tim had seen the groundhog without them!

Tim passed the picture around. It was blurry, as if the camera had moved, thought Molly. And the groundhog was very far away.

"I can't tell what this thing is," said Roger.

"It looks like it has long ears," said Rachel.

"Hey, I'll bet Tim's groundhog is a rabbit!" shouted Sonny.

Molly looked at the picture. "It looks like a groundhog to me," she said. She wanted groundhogs to be over and done with. She wanted Tim to get the badge too. He did not need to know that his groundhog was a rabbit. His feeling good was more important than the truth.

When all the groundhog talk was over, Molly showed her barbecue grill to the group. "And we used it already," she said. "It really works. Rachel helped me make it."

"You have to be careful with fire," said Mrs. Peters. "Grills can be dangerous things. Be sure your parents are there before you light it."

Molly nodded. Everyone knew fire was dangerous. She wished their leader hadn't brought that up now. It seemed to take a little of the excitement away from her project, which was perfectly safe.

"That was very inventive, Molly," said Mrs. Peters.

Molly felt better. Her feelings were more easily hurt than the others', she thought. She would have to try to be less sensitive.

Tim was waving his hand. "Guess what? I've got something better than a pool at my house! My mom said the swimming pool would make a real good garden. I shoveled the dirt back and I'm going to plant seeds there when it gets warm."

Molly wanted to give Tim a big hug. He had done it himself. He had found a way to make the pool work. But she couldn't give Tim a hug, because the others would tease her. And Tim would hate it. And Roger would call her Tim's girlfriend.

Lisa showed the Pee Wees her toothbrush holder, and Tracy showed off a painted wooden fish that could hold keys.

"What creative people are in Troop 23!" said Mrs. Peters. "And now I think it is time to give out our groundhog badges that all of you worked so hard for."

Their leader was right. The Pee Wees had worked hard. Very hard.

"Worked hard!" repeated Baby Nick from his playpen.

Mrs. Stone came downstairs with the furry little groundhog badges in her hand. The Pee Wees jumped up and down, waiting. The more badges Molly got, the more excited she was.

Mrs. Stone called out the names one by one and Mrs. Peters pinned the badges on the Pee Wees' shirts as they came up.

"This is my favorite badge," said Molly, petting the furry little groundhog. The latest badge she'd gotten was usually her favorite. Especially if there was an animal on it.

The Pee Wees did not have any good deeds to report.

"We were too busy with our badge and our unbadge," said Tracy.

"Next time," said their leader. "And now we'll have our treats."

There was a special treat today. It was a big, big cake with a badge on it. But this badge was not real. It was made of frosting. A fat and round groundhog with long whiskers was on the badge.

"Hey, I've got an eye!" shouted Roger, gobbling it down.

"I've got his leg," said Lisa.

"Here goes his tail," said Sonny, popping it into his mouth.

Molly was just glad the groundhog they were eating was frosting and not the real thing. She remembered Mrs. Peters telling them that groundhog was tasty meat—meat someone could put on a barbecue like hers!

Each scout had a big piece of cake. Nick did too. Afterward they helped clean up. Then they joined hands and sang the Pee Wee Scout song and said the Pee Wee Scout pledge.

Right in the middle of the pledge Tracy frowned and said, "What is a seven-letter word for fun?"

Everyone broke into laughter.

Roger groaned. "When is she going to finish that puzzle book?" he asked.

"This is a brand-new one," said Tracy. "My aunt just gave it to me last night."

Now all the Pee Wees moaned.

"My word starts with a *P* and it means fun."

"I know what it is," said Molly. "There's only one word it can be. The best word for fun is 'Pee Wees'!"

"Pee Wees!" shouted Nick.

Molly looked around the room at all of her friends and smiled.

Pee Wees forever, thought Molly.

# Pee Wee Scout Song
## (to the tune of
## "Old MacDonald Had a Farm")

Scouts are helpers, Scouts have fun
Pee Wee, Pee Wee Scouts!
We sing and play when work is done,
Pee Wee, Pee Wee Scouts!

With a good deed here,
And an errand there,
Here a hand, there a hand,
Everywhere a good hand.

Scouts are helpers, Scouts have fun,
Pee Wee, Pee Wee Scouts!

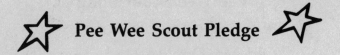

## Pee Wee Scout Pledge

We love our country
And our home,
Our school and neighbors too.

As Pee Wee Scouts
We pledge our best
In everything we do.